IF A PEACOCK FINDS A POT LEAF

Written by: Morgan Carman

Illustrated by: Geneva Carman

ISBN:1484107004
ISBN-13:9781484107003

Author's Note

I have always been taught that knowledge is the key, and in order to succeed you have to be able to decipher fact from fiction. This is why I feel it is so necessary to bring this to the forefront and teach our youth, that Medical Marijuana, and Marijuana in general is not a "drug". It is not manufactured in a lab by scientists, nor does it have the side effects that prescription drugs do. I myself am seventeen, and suffer from Social Anxiety and Obsessive Compulsive Disorder (OCD), and I find it appalling that Prescription Medications are handed out to kids like candy, only to be recalled a few months later. Yet here's a plant that is naturally grown and it is being completely overlooked for it's medicinal qualities, based on the bad reputation it's accumulated from over-hyped media on Medical Marijuana, which have created an image for 'the typical stoner'. Like any other stereotype, there are certain people who will fall into it more than others, but from what I've seen, more often than not, Medical Marijuana patients break the stereotype of 'the typical stoner'. More now than ever, people are turning to Cannabis to help them, and I believe instead of hiding it, we should engage in conversation, and openly discuss Medical Marijuana amongst ourselves, and our youth. There are so many uses for this magical plant, and the benefits are endless.

DEDICATION

This story is dedicated to
Dr. Glenn Carman and Trudy Carman.

One Day Peter the peacock was feeling a little sad, so he decided to take a walk…

But today was different, because as he was going for his walk he discovered a strange leaf in his path, and wondered what it was.

He scooped it up in his beak and carried it off with him to find his friend Benjamin Beaver.

He walked up to Benjamin Beaver and asked what the unusual leaf he'd found was. Benjamin told him it was known as Medical Marijuana, or Cannabis, and it was a very useful medicinal plant, that he himself, in fact used to help with his chronic pain from working so hard on his dam, he also told Peter of how he used the hemp plants to build the dam instead of cutting down trees, and it was helping save the other animal's environment. "There are so many uses" Benjamin assured Peter, "Ask anyone, you'll see!" Peter thanked Benjamin for the information and headed down the path, hoping to find more information about Medical Marijuana.

After he passed the river Peter came across an old owl sitting on a branch with a small white stick hanging out of her beak. She told him her name was Ophelia, and that she had Glaucoma which hurt her eyes and made it hard to catch food at night. Then she explained that rolled in the stick was Medical Marijuana. "I'm so thankful now that I have Medical Marijuana, I don't know where I would be without it." Ophelia admitted. Peter said goodbye and continued on his path.

Soon enough, along came a spider that dropped down from her web. "Hello Darling, my name is Scarlett. I've been working very hard weaving this web, and I've been waiting for someone to come admire it with me. Not long ago I suffered from such awful migraine headaches that I couldn't bear to even think of spinning such an intricate web!" Scarlett confessed. "Well what changed?" Peter asked. "I started vaporizing with Medical Marijuana, and now look at my web." I gazed at her masterpiece. "It really is something Scarlett, but I should get going." And with that Peter was back on his way...

Not too long after meeting Scarlett, Peter stumbled upon a curious creature. "I'm Cletis the Camel" he announced. "Wow, I've never seen a camel in the forest before. Where ya headed?" Peter asked. "I was just taking a walk to chew some Medical Marijuana stems so I can eat at my family reunion. They say it's a side effect to Medical Marijuana that it increases your appetite, but when you can't seem to get hungry on your own, it's helpful to have. And as for dry mouth, I got that covered!" Cletis says looking to the two humps on his back that store water. "Well I'm finally hungry, better get home." They exchanged goodbyes and Peter was back on his journey.

Peter came across the clearing right before his house, and decided to stop at the Rhino Ranch he'd passed many times.

He was greeted by an older rhino that he later learned was named Rocco. Rocco had once been a strong healthy rhino, until he was diagnosed with cancer. Rocco told Peter of how he had to undergo a harsh process called chemotherapy that left him feeling constantly nauseous. The doctors tried to treat it with prescription drugs, but nothing helped until he was recommended to smoke Medical Marijuana. It was finally something that worked without the side effects of harmful prescription drugs. Peter promised to return to the Rhino Ranch, said goodbye, and was back on his way home.

He stopped as he walked past his neighbor's house. The Four Rasta Pigs, they were known Medical Marijuana patients, but peter didn't actually know why they needed it, so he decided to stop by and ask. He knocked on the door. "Who's there mon?" One of the pigs called from behind the door. "Hello I'm Peter, the peacock from next door." They quickly opened the door and snatched Peter in.

"What can we do for ya mon?" The Four Rasta Pigs said in unison. "Well actually I was just wondering why you need Medical Marijuana, I've ran into so many creatures today that it helps, I was curious how you became patients." Peter replied. The Four Rasta Pigs took turns telling Peter of how they'd been losing sleep ever since the wolf moved in down the street. Eventually they went to a doctor and found out they had insomnia. Their doctor recommended Medical Marijuana because it was *natural* and wouldn't harm their bodies, but it would help them sleep. Peter thanked The Four Rasta Pigs for answering his questions and said goodbye.

As he was pushed out the door, a very frantic looking rabbit hopped up and Peter heard him say "Oh no! My doctor's appointment was 30-minutes ago, I'm late!" Peter wobbled over to the mysterious rabbit. "Hello Mr. Rabbit, are you lost?" Peter asked. "Oh, no, no, my name is Rupert, and I'm not lost, I'm just late, very late! I'm on my way to get my Medical Marijuana license to help with my anxiety." "Wow! Medical Marijuana helps with anxiety too!" Peter exclaimed. "It sure does! But I better be going, don't wanna keep the doctor waiting." Rupert said as he hopped off, and Peter thought of all the different creatures he'd come across that he never would have suspected were Medical Marijuana patients. He was amazed by the array of conditions it helped, and wondered if it could help him too!

As Peter watched Rupert the rabbit hop off to the Medical Marijuana Clinic he thought of how depressed he'd been lately and he decided to talk to the doctor to see if Medical Marijuana could help him feel better. It would be natural, like The Four Rasta Pigs mentioned, and wouldn't have all the side effects of prescription drugs for depression.

Peter gets his Medical Marijuana license, tries it, and finally he feels so much better! With a smile on his face he fans out his colorful wings and shows off his beautiful feathers. Peter has found a natural way to feel ok, and he is happy again thanks to Medical Marijuana!